Ghosts Be Gone!

Find out more spooky secrets about

Ghostville Elementary®

Ghostville Elementary®

Ghosts Be Gone!

by Marcia Thornton Jones
and
Debbie Dadey

illustrated by Guy Francis

A
LITTLE APPLE
PAPERBACK

SCHOLASTIC INC.
New York   Toronto   London   Auckland   Sydney
Mexico City   New Delhi   Hong Kong   Buenos Aires

ISBN 0-439-56004-7

Text copyright © 2004 by Marcia Thornton Jones and Debra S. Dadey. Illustrations copyright © 2004 by Scholastic Inc. SCHOLASTIC, LITTLE APPLE, GHOSTVILLE ELEMENTARY, and associated logos are trademarks and/or registered trademarks of Scholastic Inc.

12 11 10 9 8 7 6 5 4 3   4 5 6 7 8 9/0

Printed in the U.S.A.   40
First printing, September 2004

To Becky Rector — A great
writing friend who definitely
has all her marbles!

— MTJ

For Damon Gibson and
Heather Shutters — Best wishes
for a wonderful life together.

— DD

Contents

THE LEGEND

Sleepy Hollow Elementary School's
Online Newspaper

This Just In: Ghost Hunter in the Third Grade!

Breaking News: Lawyers, doctors, and all kinds of professionals were invited to Sleepy Hollow Elementary Career Day, but it sounds like third grader Andrew Potts has his own job plans. He wants to be a professional ghost hunter! One thing is for sure, the basement classroom is the perfect place to test his skills. Everyone has heard the stories that ghosts live down there. Maybe, just maybe, Andrew will catch one or two. . . . Stay tuned as more ghostly news develops.

Your friendly fifth-grade reporter,
Justin Thyme

1
Marbles

"Who cares what they do?" Jeff asked. He hung upside down from the monkey bars and let his arms dangle.

"Mr. Morton wants us to learn about different careers," Cassidy explained for the umpteenth time to her good friend. She sat on top of the monkey bars and swung her feet back and forth.

The third graders at Sleepy Hollow Elementary were enjoying a short recess before another guest speaker came to their basement classroom. It was career day, and they had already heard from a lawyer, a banker, and a hotel clerk.

"I don't need to know about careers," Jeff said. "I'm going to be a big-time producer and make scary movies."

Cassidy already knew what Jeff

wanted to be. After all, Jeff, Cassidy, and Nina had been friends for a long time.

Nina pushed her long black hair out of her face and perched on top of the monkey bars beside Cassidy. "Jeff is right. It wouldn't be so bad if Mr. Morton would invite an Olympic gold medalist or professional soccer player. Someone like Mia Hamm."

Nina was good at any sport she tried, but she was especially a champ when it came to soccer. Cassidy wasn't really good at running races or playing soccer. She enjoyed watching television just like most kids, but she didn't have any interest in making movies. What Cassidy really liked to do was work on her computer.

"I'll tell you who I'd like to meet," Cassidy said as she climbed down from the monkey bars. "Bill Gates, that's who! He's a computer expert and the richest man in the world."

Nina shook her head. "That'll never

happen. Instead, we have to listen to people like Andrew's dad and Carla and Darla's mom."

Jeff rolled his eyes and swung down from the bars. "Boring!" he said.

"Jeff is right," a big kid named Andrew said as he walked up and tugged on Cassidy's long, curly hair. "If you ask me, Mr. Morton is full of bad ideas, and this is one of his worst."

"Not all of Mr. Morton's ideas are bad," Cassidy told Andrew as she jerked her hair away from him.

Nina nodded. "The marble jar is a great idea."

At the beginning of the week, Mr. Morton had set a giant jar on his desk. Whenever the class was "caught" being good, Mr. Morton dropped in a marble. He promised them a pizza party when the jar was completely filled. Marbles already filled half the jar.

"The marbles are a dumb idea," Andrew said.

"We didn't ask you," Cassidy pointed out. "But since you brought it up, I think you don't like the marble jar because you never get caught being good."

"I'm good," Andrew said with a grin. "Good at causing trouble," he added.

"Well, you better not get in trouble when our next guest speaker is here," Nina said, "or Mr. Morton will take marbles out of the jar."

"I bet that's her now," Jeff said. The kids watched a short woman with a nest of gray hair hurry across the playground. She glanced over her shoulder as if to make sure nobody was following her. Then she disappeared down the steps that led directly to the kids' third-grade classroom.

"Hey, I know her," Nina said. "That's Miss Bogart. She owns the flower shop across the street from Sleepy Hollow Cemetery."

"Don't tell me we have to listen to someone explain how to pick daisies," Andrew said with a groan.

"Remember," Cassidy warned Andrew, "you have to be good so Mr. Morton will give us more marbles — no matter how boring Miss Bogart is."

"If you ask me," Andrew said, "Mr. Morton has *lost* his marbles!"

2
Miss Bogart

Mr. Morton waited until all the kids had lined up at the top of the steps that led straight down to their basement classroom. He peered at the students through his thick glasses. "Remember your manners," Mr. Morton warned. "And if everyone behaves, it will be worth five marbles!"

"Five marbles?" a girl named Carla said.

"We can do it!" her twin sister Darla added.

As the kids filed down the steps and into their classroom, Jeff, Cassidy, and Nina felt a distinct chill. They knew that could mean only one thing: ghosts.

When Sleepy Hollow Elementary had become too crowded, their classroom

had moved to the basement. Being in the basement normally wouldn't have been so bad. After all, they did have their own door that led right to the playground. But there was a legend about the basement. A legend about ghosts. That's why kids called their school Ghostville Elementary. Most people didn't really believe the stories, but Cassidy, Jeff, and Nina did. They had seen the ghosts with their very own eyes.

The air near Cassidy's desk twinkled with green flickers of light. The glittering specks swirled and thickened until they took shape. Cassidy groaned. Nina gasped, and Jeff shook his head. They knew exactly what the green haze was. Ghosts.

A boy ghost wearing overalls and a girl with a gingham dress popped into view. Cassidy, Jeff, and Nina were the only ones who could see the ghosts. The three friends had learned that ghosts could choose who saw them and who didn't. That didn't stop Cassidy from looking to make sure no one else had noticed Ozzy and his sister Becky as the kids walked past Miss Bogart on the way to their desks.

Their Career Day guest was so short

she could look most of them right in the eyes. The only thing that made her taller was the hair piled high on her head. Her face was lined with wrinkles, and she wore ten silver bracelets on her left wrist. When she moved, the bracelets clanked like a broken bell.

"We have to ignore Ozzy and Becky," Jeff hissed.

Cassidy nodded, but she knew that ignoring ghosts was about as easy as pretending chocolate wasn't sweet.

"The ghosts better behave while Miss Bogart is here," Nina whispered. "She looks old and weak. A ghostly scare might make her lose her dentures."

"I don't think we have to worry about the ghosts," Jeff said softly. "They think career day is boring, too."

Ozzy and Becky did act like they were bored. Becky floated up to the ceiling and curled up for a nap. Ozzy plopped in a trash can and yawned.

"Ozzy and Becky might be bored,"

Cassidy whispered just loud enough for Nina and Jeff to hear, "but Nate looks interested. Too interested."

Her two friends glanced above Mr. Morton's desk, where another ghost had popped into view. The kids didn't know too much about Nate. He rarely talked.

Nate weaved around the pencil container and coffee mug on Mr. Morton's desk until his face was squished up next to the marble jar. His eyeballs were magnified by the glass.

"I noticed somebody's been on the computer learning about marbles," Cassidy muttered as she slid into her seat. "I bet it was Nate."

"You mean he's been *in* the computer, don't you?" Jeff whispered. It was true. The classroom ghosts didn't use the computer like real kids. Instead, they had figured out how to ooze into the Internet cord and zoom through the wires. "That's what I call really surfing the Net," Jeff added under his breath.

Everyone, except Carla and Darla, slumped down in their seats when Miss Bogart started talking about flowers.

"Flowers are a joy," Miss Bogart sang out in a tiny, high-pitched voice. "Every single blossom has its own personality. I get to know each and every one."

Cassidy tried to act interested, but it was hard, especially when Ozzy popped out of the trash can to get a closer look at Miss Bogart. Cassidy nearly shrieked

when Ozzy sat on top of her head. Things got worse when Andrew started misbehaving, too. Andrew wiggled and Cassidy hissed at him. "Sit still," she whispered, "or Mr. Morton won't give us marbles."

Andrew stuck out his tongue at Cassidy. Then he took a piece of paper from his desk and tore off tiny bits. He rolled them into teeny-tiny balls. Then he flicked them across the aisle. *Ping.* *Ping.* *Ping.* Paper missiles hit Carla, Darla, and a girl named Barbara.

Carla jumped. Darla gasped. Barbara flicked the paper wad back.

"Stop it," Jeff warned as he knocked Andrew's paper

wads to the floor. "Don't you want to fill our marble jar?"

Andrew didn't care about marbles. He only cared about having fun, and listening to someone talk about blooms was not his idea of having fun.

Miss Bogart didn't notice Andrew. She definitely didn't see Nate counting the marbles or Ozzy playing hopscotch in front of the class. And she didn't hear Becky snoring on the ceiling, either. Instead, Miss Bogart smiled. "My shop is across the street from the cemetery," she said. "Stop by and see me anytime. Now, are there any questions?"

Jeff thunked his head on his desk when Andrew's hand shot up in the air. "Aren't you scared of ghosts?" Andrew

15

asked in his most innocent-sounding voice.

Jeff sat up straight. So did Cassidy and Nina. They knew that ghosts could decide who got to hear and see them. As far as they could tell, they were the only three kids who knew for a fact that ghosts existed in the basement of Sleepy Hollow Elementary School.

Miss Bogart laughed. It was a dainty sound that reminded Nina of delicate glass. She shivered at the thought of one of the ghosts scaring the wrinkles off Miss Bogart's face.

"Why would I be frightened of ghosts?" Miss Bogart asked.

"Because you work right across from the cemetery," Andrew said. "I bet you see lots of ghosts."

Carla raised her hand, but she didn't wait to be called on. "There are no such things . . ."

". . . as ghosts," Darla finished.

Miss Bogart smiled. When she reached

up to poke a pencil through the tangles of her hair, the bracelets on her wrist clinked.

"Not only do I believe in ghosts," Miss Bogart said. "I've seen them!"

3
Moonlighting

"I don't believe it," Andrew blurted out.

Miss Bogart didn't act like Andrew was bothering her one bit. "Believe it," she said. "In fact, I have another job. A job very different than making art out of flowers. But I hesitate to tell you about it."

"What is it?" Carla asked.

"Tell us," Darla urged.

"But you are mere children," Miss Bogart said. "I don't want to . . . frighten you."

"You can't scare me," Andrew bragged.

Miss Bogart looked long and hard at Andrew. "Perhaps," she said.

"He's right," another boy called out. "None of us is afraid."

"We can take it," Barbara added.

"What do you do?" Allison asked.

19

Mr. Morton cleared his throat, and the kids turned in their seats to hear what he had to say. "Please continue, Miss Bogart," their teacher said. "The students need to know about all types of careers."

"Very well," Miss Bogart said. "By day, I am a florist. By night, I am a professional ghost hunter!"

Everyone perked up at that, especially Cassidy, Jeff, and Nina. Even Mr. Morton looked like he had just woken up from a nap. He wiped chalk dust away from his glasses and peered at Miss Bogart.

"You're kidding!" Cassidy yelled out. Even the ghosts seemed interested. Becky flew down from the ceiling, Nate oozed off Mr. Morton's desk, and Ozzy stopped untying Miss Bogart's shoelaces. The three ghosts floated quietly in front of Miss Bogart and waited for her to say more.

"You see ghosts?" Nina blurted.

"Real ghosts?" Jeff asked.

"Cool," Andrew said. "Tell us more."

20

Miss Bogart clasped her hands as if she were praying. "Well, I've been ghost hunting ever since I was about your age. I had heard stories about ghosts and wanted to see if they were true. As a ghost hunter, I wait until the dark of night and then go into haunted houses and cemeteries in search of restless spirits."

"Why do you wait until night?" Nina asked politely.

"I have to go at night," she said. "Ghosts only make themselves known by the light of the moon."

No sooner had she said that than Ozzy hovered over

Miss Bogart. He waved at Jeff, Cassidy, and Nina. Cassidy groaned. Nina gasped and her hands started shaking. Jeff shook his head.

"Don't ghosts exist in daylight?" a girl named Allison asked.

"Definitely not," Miss Bogart said. Ozzy puffed up his cheeks and then blew into Miss Bogart's hair. Miss Bogart's hair tilted to a crazy angle, and she reached up to set it straight again.

Jeff sighed. Ozzy was playing tricks on Miss Bogart, and she didn't even know it.

"Can I go with you some night?" Andrew asked. "I want to see a ghost."

Miss Bogart laughed delicately. "Only a chosen few are able to see ghosts," she told him. "That is why I am the lone ghost hunter in the town of Sleepy Hollow. No one else has been chosen."

Ozzy reached out and poked Miss Bogart on the arm, only he didn't concentrate and his hand passed right through her skin. Ghosts have to think

very hard if they want to touch something in the real world. Miss Bogart absent-mindedly scratched at the spot on her arm.

"How do you find ghosts?" Barbara asked.

Miss Bogart winked as if she were telling a big secret. "It is no easy task, but I know how to trick a ghost. I set up cameras and catch them on film when they least expect it."

As soon as Miss Bogart mentioned cameras, Jeff sat up straight. "You can videotape a ghost?" he asked.

Miss Bogart nodded. "You can video-tape *and* photograph them."

"Like taking a picture at a birthday party?" Andrew asked.

Miss Bogart laughed for the third time. "A ghost's picture isn't quite like our own. Instead of seeing the shape of ghosts, they appear as bright lights. When I catch an orb of light on film, it is the only way I can determine if a location is truly haunted. Ghosts are extremely shy."

At that, Ozzy zoomed down to kiss Miss Bogart right on the tip of her nose!

4
The Bestest Ghost Hunter Ever

Mr. Morton rose from his desk. "Thank you for sharing information about being a florist as well as for telling such . . . um . . . interesting stories," Mr. Morton told Miss Bogart as he gently guided her to the door that led to the basement hallway. "I am sure the students were . . . er . . . entertained."

Miss Bogart smoothed her hair and smiled up at Mr. Morton. "I suppose it is my duty to the community to pass on what I know to a new generation," she said. "Perhaps I could return some other time and show them my research."

Andrew didn't bother raising his hand. "That would be great, Mr. Morton. Wait until I tell my dad that I learned how to catch ghosts!"

Mr. Morton's face grew pale. "Maybe that's not such a good idea," he said.

"Of course it isn't," Darla said. "Everyone knows . . ."

". . . there are no such things as ghosts," Carla finished.

A jingle interrupted the kids. Or maybe it was a jangle. The door to the room flew open, causing papers to scatter and Miss Bogart to gasp. A tall woman wearing red overalls blocked Miss Bogart's way.

All the kids knew exactly who it was. Olivia. In fact, almost everyone in the town of Sleepy Hollow knew her. Olivia had been the school janitor since before

most people could remember. She seemed to go with the school like peanut butter went with chocolate. Everyone liked her, even if she was a little odd. Olivia had a soft spot for everybody — including lost and homeless animals. She didn't like just the kitty-cat and puppy-dog varieties. Olivia was known for helping snakes, spiders, and even lizards if they needed her. Today, Olivia had an owl perched on her shoulder.

"Do I smell something in here?" Olivia asked. She looked at Miss Bogart's pile of hair and sniffed the air. "Something rotten?" The owl stretched its head into the air for a quick sniff. Then it hooted and tucked its head under a wing as if it had just smelled something worse than rotten cheese.

Mr. Morton looked around, too. "It can't be anything in here," he said. "Miss Bogart just finished telling about her . . . um . . . careers. We haven't cooked up anything that smells."

Olivia raised an eyebrow. "I thought something was a little stinky," she said. "Well, if you're sure . . ."

Olivia took one last look at Miss Bogart before disappearing into the gloomy depths of the hallway.

"I apologize for the interruption," Mr. Morton said.

"It is quite all right," Miss Bogart said. "Now, where was I?"

"You were just going out the door," Mr. Morton said. "Thank you for visiting."

After Miss Bogart left, Andrew waved his hand in the air until Mr. Morton finally called on him. "What is it, Andrew?" Mr. Morton asked. His voice sounded tired.

"All of us paid attention to Miss Bogart," Andrew pointed out. "We even asked good questions just like you taught us."

"Can it really be . . . ?" Darla asked.

". . . Andrew is right?" Carla added. She sounded surprised.

Mr. Morton sighed. "You did pay attention. You asked good questions. A deal is

30

a deal," he said and plopped five big marbles in the jar, making it nearly full.

Andrew pumped his fist in the air. "That pizza is almost mine!" he said. Andrew and Mr. Morton didn't see Nate, but Cassidy saw him. The quiet ghost stared at the marble jar with a huge grin on his face.

As the kids lined up at the door to go home that afternoon, they couldn't stop talking about Miss Bogart. Most of the kids still didn't believe in ghosts or ghost hunting. Of course, Nina, Jeff, and Cassidy did. They knew ghosts were real, and they knew there were ghosts in their classroom, but they didn't say a word.

"Being a ghost hunter is an awesome idea," Andrew said as their teacher led the kids outside. "It would be much more exciting than counting money for a bank or writing stories for the newspaper."

"Maybe you could write ghost stories for the newspaper instead," Carla said.

"No way! I'm not going to sit at a desk and type stories into a computer," Andrew told her. "I'm going to sleep all day and spend my nights in haunted houses and cemeteries, hunting ghosts."

"You don't honestly believe Miss Bogart is really a ghost hunter," Darla asked. "Do you?"

Andrew grinned so big the freckles on his cheeks squished together. "Not only do I believe her," he said, "but I'm going to become the youngest and bestest ghost

hunter the town of Sleepy Hollow has ever seen."

"There are no such things as ghosts," Carla reminded him.

"And there is no such word as *bestest*," Darla added.

But Andrew didn't hear them. He raced across the playground and left the rest of the third graders in his dust.

5
Marble Thief

The next morning, Cassidy, Nina, and Jeff met at the corner to walk to school together, just like they always did.

"I wonder if Andrew still wants to be a ghost hunter," Cassidy said as her sneakers crunched through a pile of dead leaves.

"He has no clue how hard it is to catch a ghost," Jeff said.

Nina nodded. She remembered trying to catch the ghosts that lived in their classroom, but Ozzy and the rest of his ghostly friends were too slippery.

The kids were barely in the classroom when Darla pointed at Mr. Morton's desk. "Ahhhhhhh!" she screamed.

"Somebody stole our marbles!" Carla added.

It was true. The jar had been nearly

full. Now half the marbles had disappeared. Everyone in the room turned and glared at Andrew, even Mr. Morton. "I didn't touch that marble jar," Andrew sputtered.

Mr. Morton sadly shook his head. "I hope whoever is responsible will do the right thing and return the marbles."

But Mr. Morton was disappointed, and so was the rest of the class. Not only did no one put the marbles back, but the next day more marbles were missing.

The day after that even more marbles disappeared. By the end of the week, only a few marbles rolled around the bottom of the jar.

"This is Jeff's fault," Andrew said. "He's trying to get me in trouble."

"Am not," Jeff argued, his cheeks turning red.

Carla and Darla pointed at Cassidy. "I bet she took them."

Cassidy faced the twins, her hands on her hips. "I would never steal the marbles. How do we know that both of you didn't do it?"

Carla gasped. Darla's hands flew up to her face. "Carla didn't steal them," Darla argued.

"Neither did Darla," her sister added.

Everyone started arguing at once. Mr. Morton cleared his throat. He clapped his hands. "Let's quiet down," he told the class. When that didn't work, Mr. Morton stood on his chair and yodeled. *"Yo-de-le-de. Yo-de-le-deeee. Yo-de-le-de-o!"*

A yodeling teacher is not something most kids see in their classroom. In fact, this was the first time Mr. Morton had tried it. The room grew silent as the kids stopped fighting, to stare at their teacher. When he was sure he had their attention, Mr. Morton wiped the chalk dust away from his glasses and peered down at the students.

"Obviously, my marvelous marble idea is not working. I'm tempted to forget the entire thing," Mr. Morton said as he hopped down to the floor.

"That means no party," Cassidy said.

"And no pizza," Andrew added.

"Exactly," Mr. Morton said. "There will be no pizza and no party unless the marbles are found!"

"What are we going to do?" Cassidy asked Nina and Jeff as they walked home from school that afternoon.

"What *can* we do?" Nina asked. "Unless we find those marbles, the pizza party is history."

"I bet our ghost friend Nate took them, and he's hiding them somewhere in the basement," Cassidy said.

"Why would Nate steal our marbles?" Nina asked.

Cassidy shrugged. "He's been staring at that jar for days," Cassidy said. "And he's been surfing the Internet looking for sites about marbles. It has to be him."

"If Nate is taking our marbles," Nina said with a sad voice, "we'll never prove it."

Jeff stopped walking. A slow grin spread across his face. "Never fear," he told his friends. "I have the perfect plan for catching our marble thief!"

6
Video Ghost

"*This* is your great idea?" Cassidy asked, shaking her head. "How is this going to help us get our marbles back?"

"We'll catch the thief on videotape," Jeff said, patting the old video camera his dad had given him.

Nina hopped across a crack in the sidewalk. It was the next morning and the kids were on their way to school. "That will never work," Nina said. "Remember what Miss Bogart said? Ghosts only show up as a ball of light on video."

"That's okay," Jeff said, doing a little dance as he crossed the street. "We'll see where the light goes, and we'll follow it to our marbles."

Cassidy grinned. "Awesome!"

"Why don't we just ask Nate where the

marbles are?" Nina asked. "I'm sure he'd give them back to us."

Jeff rolled his eyes. "You're in la-la land. Nate's never going to give up those marbles without a fight. We have to find them, unless you want to fight a ghost."

Nina shook her head, but Cassidy stopped short when they got to the school grounds. "How do we know that Nate took the marbles?" she asked her friends. "Maybe Andrew really did swipe them."

Jeff held up his video camera. "We'll find out for sure. Cameras don't lie."

It took some fast-talking on Jeff's part, but he convinced Mr. Morton to let him set up the camera. Before class began, Jeff installed the video camera in the hallway pointing toward the classroom. "I told Mr. Morton that this was part of a science experiment on hallway traffic," Jeff whispered to Cassidy.

"I hope it works," she said, pointing to the marble jar. Only two small marbles remained in the jar. "At this rate, we'll never get our pizza party."

All day long, Cassidy wondered about the video camera, especially when another marble was missing the next morning. Did the video camera catch the thief? She couldn't wait to find out, but Mr. Morton didn't give them a chance to watch the tape.

"Cassidy," Mr. Morton said as soon as he came into the room. "Would you see what's wrong with the new computer?

41

It's been acting strange." Cassidy went to the back of the room to take a look.

Strange wasn't the word. *Haunted* was more like it. Nate floated around on the screen, and nothing Cassidy could do would make him come out of the computer. Finally, in desperation, Cassidy typed, DID YOU STEAL OUR MARBLES?

Nate didn't answer, but he did make the computer screen flash on and off. By recess, Cassidy was sure Nate was the thief.

The three friends waited until the rest of their class had filed out the playground door for recess before rushing out into the hallway. Cassidy and Nina huddled close to Jeff as he rewound the tape.

"Let us see," Nina said.

"I just know Nate took those marbles," Cassidy said. "He's acting too weird."

"Look!" Nina said, pointing to the white glow on the video screen. "That's our ghost."

"Ghost?" someone said.

The three kids whirled around to find Andrew standing behind them. "What ghost?" he asked.

7
Ghost Glue

"There are no ghosts," Jeff lied.

"You just said you saw a ghost," Andrew said. "I heard you. Let me see that." He dropped the basketball he had in his hands and grabbed Jeff's video camera.

"Give that back," Nina said. "You're going to break it."

Andrew's jaw dropped as he looked at the video screen. A white ball of light floated down the hallway. A dark shadow flew past the white ball, and they both entered the basement classroom.

"It's just like Miss Bogart told us," Andrew said.

Cassidy took the camera away from Andrew. "That's doesn't mean anything. I bet it was only a smudge on the camera lens," she explained. She wiped the lens with the edge of her shirt.

Andrew shook his head and grinned. "Ghostville Elementary really *does* have a ghost. Maybe two! All I have to do is catch one and I'll be rich! I'll be a famous ghost hunter!"

"*Shh,*" Nina said, looking around to make sure no one else had come in from recess. "You can't tell anyone about this. They'll think you're crazy."

"They won't think I'm nuts when I catch this ghost," Andrew said. "I'm going to find it right now. Then I'll be on TV." Andrew took off down the hall, looking right and left and up and down.

"What about recess?" Cassidy called. "You don't want to get in trouble for being inside."

Andrew didn't answer. Getting in trouble never bothered him.

"Wait just a minute," Jeff said. "What are you going to do if you find a ghost?"

Andrew stopped to think. Then he took a piece of gum out of his pocket and chewed. Within minutes, he had blown a huge bubble. He took it out of his mouth and held it up. "This is a guaranteed ghost catcher," he said. "If a ghost comes close to this, they'll stick to it like glue. Ghost glue."

Andrew started down the hall again while Nina worried. "What will we do if he finds one of the ghosts?" she whispered.

"He won't find them," Cassidy said softly. "They'll find him. Look."

Andrew held his bubble high in the air, but he didn't see the ghosts hovering around him. Ozzy squeezed himself inside the bubble, while Nate tiptoed behind Andrew and poked him in the back. Andrew looked around, but didn't see anything.

Ozzy's little sister, Becky, and her friend Sadie held hands and danced

around Andrew. Their glowing green forms shimmered in the dim hallway light. Ozzy quickly got tired of playing in the bubble. He concentrated and with one huge poke, Ozzy popped the bubble. Bubblegum exploded all over Andrew's face and onto Ozzy. For one horrible second, Andrew saw bubblegum outlined on Ozzy's form.

"Look," Andrew screamed and lunged for Ozzy. "It's the ghost!"

8
Splat!

"That wasn't a ghost," Cassidy told Andrew. "It was gum stuck to your eyelashes."

Andrew pulled the sticky mess from his face and hair. "I don't believe you. It was a ghost, and now it's made me mad. That ghost is going to be sorry it ever laid its beady eyeballs on Andrew T. Johnson."

"I know *I'm* sorry," Nina said.

Andrew ignored Nina and stomped into the classroom. He came back into the hall with his arms loaded. He had big bottles of white glue, a jar of paste, a pencil, and three jars of fluorescent paint. "All right, ghosts!" Andrew roared. "Show yourselves now, unless you're scaredy-ghosts."

Ghosts must love a dare, because green sparkles filled the air. In minutes, the air in the hallway filled with ghosts that Andrew couldn't see. Not only did Ozzy, Nate, Becky, and Sadie appear, but their friends Calliope and Edgar came out of nowhere, too. Even Ozzy's dog, Huxley, ran up to sniff Andrew's sneakers, and Calliope's cat, Cocomo, twirled between Andrew's feet.

When Huxley lifted his leg next to Andrew's knee, Cassidy screamed and scared Huxley away. "Andrew!" she said. "What are you going to do with all that?"

"If I squirt this stuff around, it's sure to land on a ghost. Then I'll be able to see him," Andrew explained.

"Do you think that will really work?" Nina asked.

"The gum worked a little bit," Andrew

said. "Stand back and let me take action." Andrew squirted glue through the air. He threw paste against the wall. Then he unscrewed the paint.

"Stop!" Cassidy yelled. "You can't throw paint in school!"

"When I catch those ghosts, everyone will thank me," Andrew said. "Besides, it's water-based paint. It'll wash off."

"No!" Nina screamed. She ran up to stop Andrew just as he tossed green paint at the wall. Bright paint splattered Nina from top to bottom.

"Oooohhhhh!" Nina screamed. "Look what you've done! Are you insane?"

Cassidy ran to the bathroom to get paper towels and dabbed them on Nina's shirt. "Does she look like a ghost to you?" Cassidy snapped at Andrew.

"Forget it," Andrew said. "I'll just poke that ghost into surrendering." Andrew held up his sharp pencil and stabbed it into the air.

A terrible squeak came from the end of the hall, and Jeff feared that maybe Andrew had hurt one of the ghosts. A huge dark shadow loomed over the kids. Andrew dropped his pencil and screamed.

9
Waking the Dead

"Olivia!" Jeff gasped. The tall shadow belonged to their janitor, and she definitely didn't look happy. Her earrings jingled and jangled as she stared at the paint and glue on the floor. The small owl on her shoulder flapped its wings. The ghosts were nowhere to be seen.

"Alex Owl and I want to know what's going on here," Olivia told the kids.

"Um," Cassidy said.

"'Um' is all you have to say?" Olivia asked. "You kids are in big trouble! First of all, you're supposed to be outside. Second of all, you're being so loud you could wake the dead."

"That's exactly what I want to do," Andrew explained. "I'm ghost hunting!"

Olivia laughed out loud. "You wouldn't recognize a ghost if it came up and said howdy-do," she told Andrew.

The owl on Olivia's shoulder hooted. "It's all right, Alex," Olivia said, petting the bird. "I'll get them to clean up this mess."

Olivia pointed to the paste and paint splattered on the floor and wall. "Get busy," she ordered the kids.

"But we didn't do it!" Jeff sputtered.

Olivia laughed again. "Next, I suppose you'll be telling me a ghost was finger painting out here. Get busy, and then get out of this hallway. From now on, I want you to be quiet. Very quiet. You're disturbing Alex's beauty sleep."

Cassidy opened her mouth to tell Olivia that this was all Andrew's fault, but Olivia jingled and jangled down the hall without a backward glance. The owl hooted once, and then everything was quiet.

Jeff pointed a finger at Andrew. "This is your mess. You clean it up."

"Me?" Andrew said. "I'm supposed to be at recess." Andrew grabbed his basketball and took off toward the door leading to the playground.

"Get back here!" Nina yelled, but it didn't do any good. Andrew was gone.

"I can't believe him!" Cassidy snapped and stomped her foot.

"*Shh!*" Jeff said. "Before Olivia comes back."

Nina mopped up the paint with paper towels. "I know one thing," she said. "If Andrew did catch the ghosts, it would be

terrible. He'd probably keep them locked in a cage and charge fifty cents to see them."

Cassidy nodded and picked up a blob of paste. "Andrew has to be stopped before it's too late."

10
Foolproof

Stopping Andrew was like trying to stop a roller coaster from flying down a hill, especially when the last marble in the jar turned up missing the next morning.

Jeff, Nina, and Cassidy gathered in the hallway when the rest of the kids left for art class. They thought they were alone, but just as Jeff started the videotape from the night before, Andrew galloped down the steps and pushed his way into their huddle.

"There," Andrew said, pointing to a bright light floating down the darkened hallway on the tiny screen of the camera. "That's the marble-stealing ghost!"

"You can't really believe in ghosts,"

Nina said, but her voice sounded small and unsure.

"Of course I do," Andrew said. "Miss Bogart makes a living hunting ghosts. Which is exactly what I'm going to do, and I plan to get started by catching the ghosts that lurk in the shadows of our basement."

"You can't catch a ghost," Jeff said. "You already tried."

"All you managed to do was ruin my new shirt," Nina said.

"And get us in trouble," Cassidy added.

Andrew tapped his head with his finger. "I've been thinking."

"Uh-oh," Cassidy said.

"That can't be good," Nina said.

"Very funny," Andrew said with a sneer. "But this time, my idea is foolproof."

"If you mean your idea is proof that you're a fool, then I believe you," Jeff said.

"No," Andrew said, "my idea is going to make me famous. And being the nice guy that I am, I'm going to let you in on it. All you have to do is show up at the playground. Tonight. At midnight."

"Midnight?" Nina squeaked.

Andrew nodded. "Midnight is the best time of all to spot a ghost, so that's when we're going to sneak into the basement and catch that ghost."

"I'm not allowed to go outside after dark," Nina said. "And neither are you."

"This is an emergency," Andrew said. "Rules don't count. I'll see you at midnight!" He didn't wait to hear another word. He turned and stomped up the steps, leaving Cassidy, Jeff, and Nina in the basement alone.

"Do you really think one of the ghosts is stealing our marbles?" Nina asked.

Cassidy nodded. "Nate told us a long time ago he'd lost his special birthday marble," she said. "He's been using the computer to find out everything he can about marbles. It makes sense that he's our thief."

"I want our marbles back," Nina said, "but I don't want Nate to get hurt."

"What if Andrew catches Nate?" Jeff asked.

"Whatever it takes," Cassidy said grimly, "we can't let that happen."

11
At the Stroke of Midnight

Clouds drifted across the moon and blocked the stars from sight as Cassidy, Jeff, and Nina made their way to the playground that night. Wind hissed through dried leaves, and in the distance, a dog howled. Nina shivered, and it wasn't from the cold.

"This is wrong," she said. "We shouldn't be doing this."

"We can't let Andrew catch Nate," Cassidy said. "He'll tell everyone about the classroom ghosts."

"So what?" Jeff said. "Nobody would believe him, anyway."

"But we'd have to listen to Andrew fighting with the ghosts for the rest of the year," Cassidy pointed out. "There would be no peace at Ghostville Elementary."

"Cassidy is right," Jeff said. "Andrew and ghosts don't mix. Ozzy causes enough mischief. What if the two of them got together? There's no telling how much trouble they'd cause. We have to keep them apart."

"Then let's get this over with," Nina told them, "so we can go home and get to bed before we're caught!"

The kids silently made their way across the playground. The chains on the swing set creaked in the wind, and the monkey bars cast a black shadow where Andrew was waiting.

"It's about time," Andrew said. "I was beginning to think you were too chicken to come."

"I'm not scared," Jeff said.

"Neither am I," Cassidy said.

Nina didn't say a word.

"Let's go catch ourselves a ghost," Andrew said. Just then the clouds drifted

away from the moon long enough for the kids to see that Andrew was carrying a huge net.

"What is that?" Nina asked. "It looks like the net from a soccer goal."

Andrew held the net in front of him. "It was," he said, "but now it is an Andrew-patented ghost-catching device."

"I don't think you can catch a ghost with a net," Cassidy said. She knew the net would go right through a ghost, but Andrew wasn't listening.

"The school is bound to be locked up tighter than a bank vault," Nina pointed out. "We might as well just forget about this."

When Andrew grinned, his teeth showed up white in the moonlight. "I told you I had this plan worked out," he said. "Now, follow me."

Without another word, Andrew led the way around the back of the school. The kids' feet crunched leaves as they went. Something squeaked and scurried out of their way just as Nina walked through a spiderweb.

"Spiders!" Nina shrieked. "I *hate* spiders."

"*Shh*," Cassidy warned, wiping the web from Nina's long, black hair.

Nina whimpered and hid behind Cassidy. "You go first," Nina said.

Andrew stopped in front of a basement window. He carefully removed a twig he had used to prop it open. "Follow me," he whispered. He slowly crawled inside.

Cassidy looked at Jeff. Jeff looked at Nina. Nina looked at them both. "It's now or never," Cassidy finally said.

She silently crawled into the basement window after Andrew. Nina and Jeff followed.

The four kids waited beneath the window until their eyes adjusted to the deep shadows. They were standing at the end of the long basement hall outside their classroom. Jeff noticed the red light of his camera pointed toward the classroom

door. It looked like a bloody eye peering through the darkness.

"This way," Andrew whispered.

It was so dark, the kids had to hold hands so they wouldn't get separated. Andrew led them to a stack of boxes. "This will be a perfect place for us to watch from," Andrew said.

The kids hunkered down behind the boxes. Minutes ticked by. The wind outside scraped a branch against the bricks, sounding like fingernails screeching across a chalkboard.

Cassidy yawned. Nina shivered. Jeff's leg went to sleep. "This isn't working," Jeff said.

"We can't sit here forever," Cassidy agreed.

"I think we should go home," Nina added. "Nothing is going to happen."

Then the church bells down the street chimed twelve times. It was exactly midnight.

The door at the top of the steps leading to the rest of the school slowly creaked open. Nina grabbed Cassidy's arm.

Cassidy held her breath. Jeff got ready to run. Not Andrew. He gripped his net.

A slow tap-tap-tapping sound made its way down the steps. Suddenly, a bright light flashed in their direction.

"It's the ghost!" Andrew shouted.

12
Ghost Evidence

Andrew jumped up from his hiding spot and threw his giant net over the light. It was a light, all right. A flashlight! And it was held by none other than Miss Bogart. She was so surprised to see the kids, she screamed.

The kids were so surprised to see her, they screamed, too. *"Ahhhhhh!!!!"*

As Andrew pulled the net off Miss Bogart, light flooded the hallway. "What is going on here?" Olivia yelled.

Miss Bogart switched off her flashlight and her cheeks turned red. "I know I'm not supposed to be here."

"You're right about that," Olivia said with a frown. Her earrings jingled and jangled as she looked at the kids. They all put their heads down and hoped Olivia would forget about them.

"I must admit that I've always wondered if the legends about the basement being haunted were true," Miss Bogart explained. "Up until this year I couldn't find out because the basement had been boarded up. I didn't realize it had been reopened until Mr. Morton asked me to come speak to his class."

"That's when you realized you could do a little ghost hunting of your own?" Cassidy asked.

Miss Bogart nodded. "I've been coming every night, looking for evidence of ghosts."

"Did you find any?" Andrew asked anxiously.

Miss Bogart opened her mouth to answer. But instead of speaking, she screamed.

Something swooped down and snatched at the pile of hair on Miss Bogart's head. "Alex, no!" Olivia yelled at her owl.

The kids ducked. Miss Bogart screamed again as the owl grabbed her hair. With silent wings, Alex took off down the hallway with her hair in his talons.

"It's a wig!" Cassidy shouted.

"I'm so sorry," Olivia told Miss Bogart.

Nina looked at the smile on Olivia's face and decided she wasn't really that sorry.

Olivia's earrings jingled as she explained, "Alex has been using my office as a home for the last week or so. He likes to go hunting at night. I'll be right back with your . . . er . . . hair."

Olivia rushed down the hall. The kids tried not to laugh when Olivia came back and plopped the wig on Miss Bogart's head.

"Now then, did you find any evidence of ghosts?" Olivia asked politely as Miss Bogart straightened her hair.

"No!" Miss Bogart snapped. "Sleepy Hollow Elementary is officially ghost-free."

Andrew groaned. "Then who has been stealing the marbles?"

Olivia cleared her throat. "I have the answer to that. I found these in Alex's nest." She pulled handfuls of marbles from her overall pockets.

"You mean the legend of the Ghostville Ghosts is just one big fairy tale?" Andrew asked.

Miss Bogart nodded so hard her wig nearly slipped off her head. "I'm afraid so," she said.

But Jeff, Cassidy, and Nina knew Miss Bogart was wrong because just then Ozzy, Nate, and all the other ghosts appeared in the air above Miss Bogart's wig.

Cassidy felt very bad for thinking that

Nate was stealing marbles. "May I have those marbles?" she asked Olivia. "I know someone who will take care of them for us."

Olivia handed over the marbles. "I'm sure you know what's best. Now, I hope this puts those ghost stories to rest once and for all."

Andrew sighed. "I guess you're right. There are no such things as ghosts."

"At least, not in the basement of Sleepy Hollow Elementary!" Miss Bogart agreed.

Ozzy winked at the three friends, and then, very slowly, he reached out for Miss Bogart's wig.

Ready for more spooky fun?
Then take a sneak peek at the next

Ghostville Elementary®

#9 Beware of the Blabbermouth!

Jeff didn't notice that the rest of the class was clustered at the front of the room. Cassidy did. She tugged on Jeff's sleeve until he stopped talking. Jeff slowly turned to see another message scratched in blue letters across Mr. Morton's flip chart.

JEFF IS SCARED OF BUNNIES

Andrew hopped around Jeff. "Look out!

My little bunny whiskers might poke you to death," Andrew said between laughs.

Jeff remembered looking up movies on the classroom computer a few days ago when everyone else was finishing their double-digit multiplication problems. A poster for an old movie called *Killer Rabbit* had popped up on the screen so suddenly it had startled him. He might have jumped a little bit, but nobody had seen him. Nobody.

Mr. Morton clapped his hands until the class stopped laughing. "Some species of rabbits can get rather large," their teacher started to say.

"Like the Easter bunny!" Andrew finished for their teacher.

The class burst into laughter again. This time, no amount of clapping could make them stop.

Darla rushed to the chart. "Let us . . ."

". . . help," Carla said. Then they both reached up and ripped the page from the chart.

Mr. Morton gave the twins his biggest smile. "If everyone could be half as helpful as Carla and Darla, we would never have these problems," he said as he gave the girls each a star sticker.

Nina sighed. She couldn't help but notice Edgar oozing out of the picture on the wall to follow Carla and Darla. Usually she worried that the ghosts would bother the other kids, but for once she didn't care. She watched Edgar hover over the two girls as they carefully placed the new stickers on the covers of their journals. Nina knew Edgar liked journals. He held his own tattered journal to his chest.

The rest of the ghosts couldn't care less about journals. They seemed to think the idea of Jeff being afraid of a bunny was funny. Becky hopped around Jeff's desk. Ozzy leaped through the air with his hair stuck up like rabbit ears. He looked more like a clumsy frog than a cute bunny. Even Sadie tried bouncing around the room.

Jeff's face turned from white to pink to red.

"Your red face won't match your pink bunny nose," Andrew teased. "Hey, will you give me extra chocolate eggs for Easter?"

The rest of the class laughed even harder. Mr. Morton, however, was not amused. "If this happens again," he warned, "nobody will get recess. And I mean NO ONE!"

That was enough to quiet the class. Everyone except the ghosts. They still hopped around the room. Jeff sent Ozzy tumbling with a wave of his hand when the ghost landed on Jeff's desk.

"Ignore them," Nina whispered to Jeff.

"Maybe they'll go away," Cassidy added, but she didn't sound very sure.

They all should've known better. There was one thing Ozzy did not like.

Being ignored.

About the Authors

Marcia Thornton Jones and Debbie Dadey got into the *spirit* of writing when they worked together at the same school in Lexington, Kentucky. Since then, Debbie has *haunted* several states. She currently *haunts* Ft. Collins, CO, with her three children, two dogs, and husband. Marcia remains in Lexington, KY, where she lives with her husband and two cats. Debbie and Marcia have fun with spooky stories. They have scared themselves silly with *The Adventures of the Bailey School Kids* and *The Bailey City Monsters* series.